To Je~

Drea~

Mr Fajer

Special thanks to my supportive wife who helped me every step of the way.

And to Sarah Lobb who is the reason this book is in your hands.

Orion

A story of courage and bravery

One autumn evening, a gust of wind stretched through a long winding valley.

Standing at the edge of a large canyon, the green and brown leaves of a lonely tree rustled as a howl of wind echoed in the distance.

Sitting on a branch of the solitary tree, a small owl called Orion sat with his siblings on top of a lovely warm nest. They were as snug as a bug in a rug. "How warm and perfect!" Orion thought.

Cheerful Orion was right in the middle. He had beautiful, fluffy white and brown feathers.

His older, larger brother had already grown long brown feathers however his sister was still smaller than Orion and still very fluffy.

At this time, Mother owl was not at the nest. She was out hunting, making sure the owl family was never hungry. During the day, Mother owl would swoop to the nest with some lovely grubs. "Worms, flies, grubs and bugs!" she would exclaim as she landed gracefully, "Dinner is served!" Orion was very happy.

One day, Mother owl returned, "How grown up you all are!" She smiled and looked at the three siblings who had all grown some beautiful long feathers, "You will soon be brave, strong, quick and cunning just like me."

She smiled at Orion happily, "When that day comes, you will leave the nest and find your own food."

Orion did not like the sound of this. He had heard strange howls in the evenings and had seen other, stranger birds flying around the valley. He was sure to become food for something else!

So, Orion decided it would be safer to stay in the nest and he snuggled in even closer next to Brother owl and Sister owl.

However,
the days soon became
colder and
shorter.

As promised, Mother owl had stopped visiting the little owl family and, just as Orion's tummy rumbled, Brother owl spoke,

"I am leaving to find worms, flies, grubs and bugs for myself. Nothing will be able to hurt me as I am just like Mother, brave and strong."

A piercing sun shone brightly through Brother owl's long brown wings as he gave one large, powerful flap before swooping up and out of the lonely tree.

"I am not leaving this nest!" said Orion, thinking once again of all the things that could eat him.

Shortly after Brother owl had gone, Orion's tummy rumbled once more. He gazed over at Sister owl who, after all these weeks, had grown her beautiful long, chocolate-coloured feathers. A nervous grin crept over her before she tweeted bravely, "I too am leaving to find worms, flies, grubs and bugs for myself. Nothing will be able to hurt me as I am just like Mother, quick and cunning."

Orion was sad to see her leave but watched carefully as Sister owl took her first flight under the glistening evening sun.

His tummy rumbled once more. "I am not leaving this nest." This time he thought of how he would surely get lost on his own.

The winter sun shrank in the distance, replaced by the most beautiful moon. "Maybe Mother will return..." he thought hopelessly. The stars twinkled like diamonds in the cloudless sky and the night became still and quiet. The small owl sat alone.

The morning was bitter and cold. Orion's tummy rumbled once more as he awoke alone in the nest. He thought about his brother and sister. Where could they possibly be now? "I bet they aren't as hungry as me in this silly old nest," Orion hooted as he shivered, "I think it is time I did something."

Stretching out his little twig leg, for the first time in his life, he stepped out of the nest and onto the long, sturdy branch that held up his home.

"I am leaving to find worms, flies, grubs and bugs for myself. Nothing will be able to hurt me as long as I will be like my family, brave, strong, quick and cunning." With one thrash of his wings the little owl lifted from his perch.

He took a quick breath of the cold air and began to flutter his wings and a quiver his tail...

Orion had taken flight.

Soon he was gliding down and away from the lonely tree, wind gushing through his feathers. "Brave, strong, quick and cunning," he thought as he spotted some wriggling worms on the ground.

The swooping owl tilted his feathers and flew softly past a muddy patch in the canyon, snatching the tastiest grub he had ever eaten.

Twisting and turning through the air, Orion caught all the grubs he could eat. He was the happiest owl in the world that day and he finally believed in himself.

The End

In Greek myth, Orion was a mighty
hunter who was turned into a
constellation by Zeus, King of the
Greek gods.

On a clear night, you may even be
able to see the shape in the stars,
start by looking for Orion's belt.

The Greeks also considered Orion to
mean "Rising in the sky" or "Dawning".

Orion's belt

Orion

By
RJ Frazer

Printed in Great Britain
by Amazon

77772078R00016